All rights reserved. No part of this publication
may be reproduced or transmitted, in any form
or by any means, without permission.

First published 1988 by
MACMILLAN CHILDREN'S BOOKS
A division of Macmillan Publishers Limited
London and Basingstoke
Associated companies throughout the world.

British Library Cataloguing in Publication Data
Fuge, Charles
Bush Vark's day out.
I. Title
823'.914 [J]   PZ7

ISBN 0-333-46280-7

Printed in Hong Kong

BUSH VARK'S FIRST DAY OUT

Charles Fuge

MACMILLAN CHILDREN'S BOOKS

It was a fine morning.

At the edge of the forest there was a burrow, and at the mouth of the burrow was a young bush vark.

He looked up at the sky, he looked at the trees and the plants. What strange and wonderful things there are in the world, he thought.

He sniffed the air. And what strange and wonderful smells.

Yes, this was the day he would explore. This was the day he would go outside into the world.

But he was not alone.

The bush vark trotted into the forest. Soon he came to a clearing. In the clearing were some curious animals – large ones, small ones, animals with big eyes, animals with spots and animals with spiky backs, animals with lots of teeth and animals with none.

They looked hungrily at the bush vark.

The bush vark looked at them.

At that moment, a fat pink creature stretched out a long skinny arm.

I wonder what that tastes like, thought the bush vark.

But he never found out. As the vark's teeth bit into the arm, the fat pink creature yelped and scuttled off into the forest.

Ahead of the vark was a cave.

"What an enormous burrow!" he exclaimed and hurried to look inside.

It was dark in the burrow and he couldn't see anything. But he could feel huge hairy paws clutching at him.

Fortunately, bush varks are slippery creatures. As the paws tightened their grip, he shot upwards. Before he knew what was happening he was caught – up and away

He did not come down again.

When he opened his eyes, he found himself upside down among fluttering wings and bright blinking eyes.

The vark wished he had wings too. He wriggled and flapped so much that the bats could hold him no longer. He fell and, with a splash, he landed in a deep dark pool at the bottom of a cave.

The water was warm. As the vark swam, it became clearer and brighter.

He watched the little fish darting around among the seaweed.
He was about to chase after them, when…

…he was out of the water watching the waves below grow smaller and smaller.

The huge bird flapped to a halt and the vark tumbled into her nest.
The chicks snapped their beaks and pecked at the young vark. He had fun hopping this way and that to avoid them, but the nest was not as strong as it looked…

Oops! As he toppled off the edge he saw, out of the corner of his eye, something fat and pink far below.

It was a comfortable landing for the vark, but very uncomfortable for the fat pink creature.

"This burrow looks familiar," he said, yawning. "I think it's time for bed. Exploring the world is a very tiring business."